PLAGUE

To Jack and Tom, with love always–JF.

For all the farmers who help feed us regardless of plague, flood or fire–BW.

A Scholastic Press book from Scholastic Australia

PLAGUE

JACKIE FRENCH BRUCE WHATLEY

Long ago our tribe was small.
Our nymphs grew plump
below the grasslands

where women ground grass seeds for flour.

Men hunted kangaroos

and white ibis hunted us.

The ibis nested in the
swamps and marshes,
but enough of us still grew,
and flew,
munching at the green.

We were never too many.
The world was balanced then.

Two hundred years ago
the farmers came,
they ringbarked trees and burnt them.
They drained the ibis swamps.

Fifty years ago the ibis had become
'bin chickens', scavenging stale pizzas in the cities.

Grass- and wheat-lands spread to the horizon,
and so did we, with too few ibis to control us.

We could rage across the land.

We ate the grass, the leaves, the wheat.

We were so many that
in desperation and starvation
we ate green hoses,
washing on the lines.
We left bare ground behind.

Then men fought back.

This is the story of today . . .

When poison rains from a blue sky,
the poison kills us and the bush birds that eat our bodies.

If the poison comes at the right time,
we don't become an army
but stay few,
to breed again.

Every year, the grasslands grow.

Every year, more poison must be spread

on birds and animals and people down below.

Sometimes I hear the
ancient voices laugh.
Other times
I hear them cry.

Long ago, people knew how Country must be cherished.

If you listen, you can hear
the whispers still . . .

‘You do not need poison.
You only need to understand.’

JACKIE FRENCH

More than 200 years ago, Australia didn't have locust plagues, even though it had grasslands, harvested by Indigenous farmers for the seeds. The white ibis that bred in swamps and marshlands kept the locusts under control.

One mob of ibis can eat two tonnes of locusts a week. A single ibis can eat 700 locusts a day. Other birds eat locusts too, though not in such great numbers: magpies, ravens, kestrels, kites, ducks, herons, as well as introduced birds such as sparrows, hens and turkeys.

By about 1830, the swamps were being drained. Sheep and cattle tramped the soil and made it too densely packed for the marshes that the ibis liked. Vast areas of land were cleared—to create more open grasslands or to plant cereal crops for locusts to eat. There were fewer birds to eat the locusts. There may be more ibis now than ever before in Australia, but instead of eating locusts the great mobs have moved to the cities where they are called 'bin chickens', eating stale fish and chips, or pizza and other garbage.

The first recorded swarm of the migratory locust (Locusta migratoria, the most damaging of Australia's locust species) was in 1844. By the 1870s, local plagues of locusts were common; by the 1920s, locust plagues spread for hundreds or thousands of kilometres, and lasted for as long as two years.

A locust swarm may contain millions of locusts and can cover an area of several square kilometres. If the wind is in the right direction, a swarm can fly several hundred kilometres in just a few nights, suddenly appearing and devastating an area before the farmers even realise the swarm is there. One locust eats about 0.2 grams of green vegetation per day. A one-square-kilometre swarm can consume over 1,000 kilograms a day.

Spring droughts may kill locust hatchlings, and summer droughts can prevent most of the females from having enough food to mature their eggs. Mostly, locusts are now controlled by spreading pesticides from planes, over thousands of square kilometres of farmland.

That's a lot of poison. There is no poison that harms only locusts. Some pesticides are deadly to bees

(without bees, most of our food crops won't grow). Others kill the birds and insects that help control the locusts.

Even today, we can control locusts without killing other species.

In 1984, when Australia had its worst locust plague, I was an orchardist. All around us, everything green was eaten, even garden hoses and washing on the line—but not our orchards or vegetable crops. Locusts don't like eucalypt trees, and our crops were surrounded by swathes of bush. We used micro-jet irrigation to keep the locusts from the young trees. Farmers from all around came to wonder at our lush area of green.

We had chooks too. Chooks love locusts. Our chooks leapt like ballerinas—snatching locusts from the air—and grew fat. When the locusts were resting at night, I used a vacuum cleaner on a friend's paddock, and made fertiliser from the locusts I collected. They also make great plant food. Locusts can even be made into food for humans or stock.

There are many other ways to control locusts: with fungi, natural barriers; by running free-range hens and turkeys, by nurturing more wetlands, and using giant vacuum cleaners that turn pests into rich fertiliser.

Spreading poison from the air is a rapid solution to control locusts, but effective management is cheaper and safer than poison. Humans can out-think locusts—if we only try

BRUCE WHATLEY

Plague was illustrated solely in Rebelle 5, an incredible digital watercolour painting program. I use a Mac Mini connected to a Wacom Pen Display and a large BenQ screen. An ideal set up for this kind of work. I relied heavily on historic photos and film to make the content as realistic as possible.

Scholastic Press
An imprint of Scholastic Australia Pty Limited (ABN 11 000 614 577)
PO Box 579 Gosford NSW 2250
www.scholastic.com.au

Part of the Scholastic Group
Sydney • Auckland • New York • Toronto • London • Mexico City
New Delhi • Hong Kong • Buenos Aires • Puerto Rico

Published by Scholastic Australia in 2023.

A catalogue record for this book is available from the National Library of Australia

ISBN: 978-1-74383-482-4

Typeset in Impression.
Book design by Nicole Stofberg.
Bruce Whatley created these illustrations digitally using Rebelle 5.

Printed in China by RR Donnelley.
Scholastic Australia's policy, in association with RR Donnelley, is to use papers that are renewable and made efficiently from wood grown in responsibly managed forests, so as to minimise its environmental footprint.

10 9 8 7 6 5 4 3 2 24 25 26 27 / 2

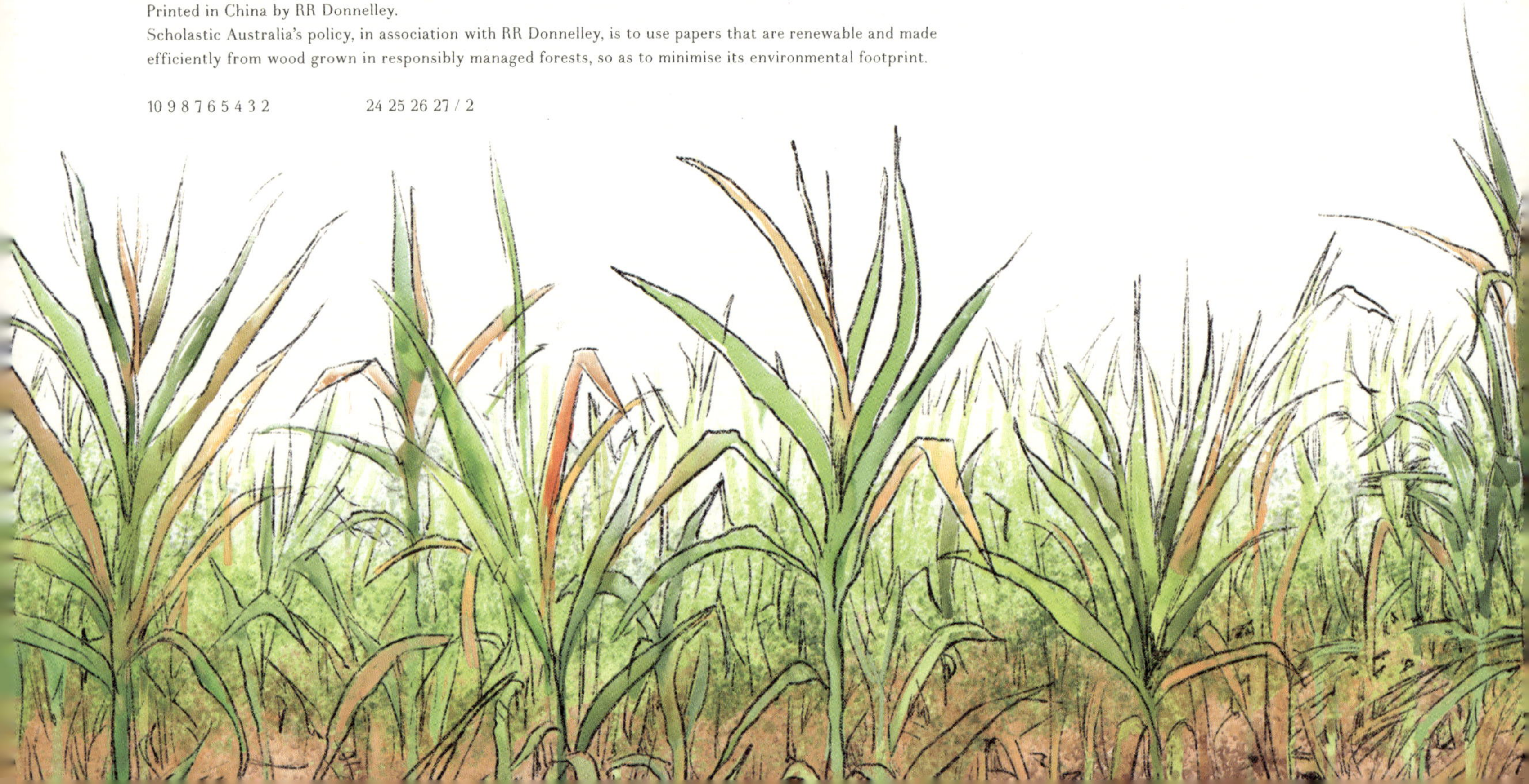